100
Days of Fun
at School

A First-Start® Easy Reader

This easy reader contains only 59 different words, repeated often to help the young reader develop word recognition and interest in reading.

100	day	Kate	things
100th	days	look	this
a	do	many	to
and	does	of	Tom
at	eat	read	too
back	for	school	treats
Bob	fun	see	very
book	giant	so	way
bring	hooray	special	we
brings	in	steps	what
can	is	take	which
come	it	that	will
cool	it's	the	words
count	jacks	them	you
counting	jumping	then	

100
Days of Fun at School

by Janet Craig

illustrated by Rebecca McKillip Thornburgh

SCHOLASTIC INC.

New York Toronto London Auckland Sydney
Mexico City New Delhi Hong Kong Buenos Aires

ISBN 0-439-68870-1

12 11 10 9 8 7 6 5 4 3 2 1   4 5 6 7 8 9/0

Printed in the U.S.A.   08

First Scholastic printing, September 2004

Hooray!
It's a very special day
for counting in a special way.

Which special day is very cool?

It's the day that we will bring 100 of so many things.

Look at Bob.
What does
Bob bring?

Is it 100?

Count and see.

Hooray! Bob brings 100.

Look at Kate.
What does Kate bring?

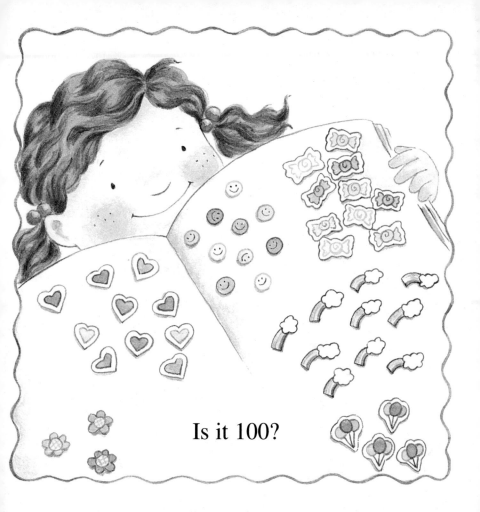

Is it 100?

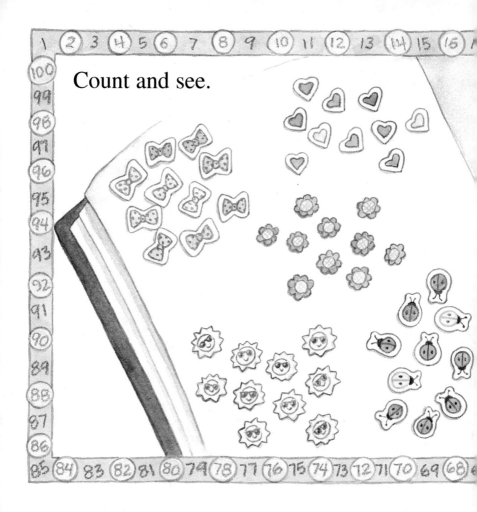

Count and see.

Hooray! Kate brings 100.

Look at Tom.
What does Tom bring?

Is it 100?

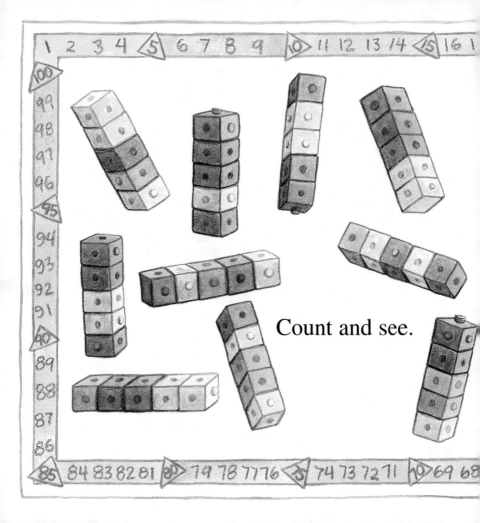

Count and see.

Hooray! Tom brings 100.

Hooray! This special day is cool.
It's the 100th day of school.

It's the day that we will do
100 things. Come do them, too.

We do 100 jumping jacks.

We take 100 giant steps . . .

and then we take 100 back.

We read 100 words, and look!
We read a special "100 Book."

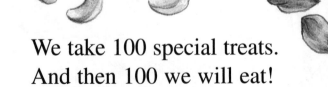

We take 100 special treats.
And then 100 we will eat!

Hooray! This special day is cool.
It's the 100th day of school!

Can you count to 100, too?

Hooray for you!